NIGHT IN THE AFTERNOON AND OTHER EROTICA

BY CAROLINE LAMARCHE

TRANSLATED FROM THE FRENCH BY HOWARD CURTIS

Grove Press
New York

Printed in the United States of America

Night in the afternoon / by Caroline Lamarche ; translated by
  Howard Curtis.

ISBN 0-7394-1279-5

CONTENTS

NIGHT IN THE AFTERNOON

I don't have any memory of my childhood. Any memory at all. Except this. I'm alone in a little bed, lying the wrong way up, my head knocking against the bottom of the bed, deep beneath the sheets, and I'm choking, because I can't find the way out, and I cry for help, I'm choking, I'm going to die, I cry for help. Downstairs, in the big drawing room, there's a reception, noises of conversation, the tinkling of glasses, nobody can hear me. But in the corridor, the maid passes. She hears a faint sound, like the whimpering of a kitten, comes in, sees the hump in the bed, and throws back the covers, like the curtain in a theater. I am saved.

1

The kittens were born three days ago. And for three days I've been bleeding. Four days, in fact—the day before the kittens were born, when I got up from the bed in that short-stay hotel, in that room I'm going to have to talk about, I saw a little drop of blood on the sheet, so light it was already dry, caused, I guess, by one of those things he used to penetrate me.

"There's a bit of blood," I said, utterly surprised, as if suddenly discovering that I had lost my virginity.

I folded the corner of the sheet, thinking of the manageress. She was a beautiful woman still, but fierce-looking, authoritarian, and I didn't want her to notice the blood. I wanted her to rip the sheet off the bed, roll it into a ball, and throw it into the washing machine with the others, all smelling of sperm and sweat—the rooms were all taken that afternoon, we were the last to arrive—and then boil the sheets slowly and throw them into a scorching hot dryer, until they were light and soft again, just things to sleep on.

When the kittens came out, they were huddled together in a sticky pouch. Then their mother tore it, and out they slid, wet and blind. Their mother—I call her Douce—is black and white, like my childhood maid, with her black dress, white apron, and white gloves, all childhood maids are black and white, there's nothing else to distinguish them, you can't tell from their faces how old they are, or what they have under their skirts, or what their feet or arms look like. But they carried me the way a mother cat carries her young, instinctively, and just as a kitten forgets its mother, so I forgot them. That's how motherhood should be—a story of maids and young masters, happy in the knowledge that you don't belong to each other, and that the kisses and the blows won't be a burden, happy that you owe your life to an anonymous hand in a white glove, and you don't have to spend your whole life blessing it or biting it.

The man had a white glove too, a white latex glove. I saw it afterwards, when the two hours were up and I was looking on the floor for my clothes. A short glove, the kind maids used to wear. It was on the floor, on the not very clean carpet, along with flesh-colored dildos and colored plastic clothespins and other things I preferred not to examine too closely. I didn't even see the strap, it must have been wide, as wide as a belt, maybe it was a big belt with a buckle, because of the two distinct scars I had, like razor cuts, one to the left of my navel and the other on my right breast.

"I used something wide," he told me later. "I didn't want to leave too much of a mark, because of your boyfriend."

Back home, it hurt a lot when I peed. There was a sharp burning sensation, and blood in the bowl. Although it was a hot day, I felt so cold that I filled the bathtub with very hot water, and when I started washing myself, I couldn't stop.

You mustn't touch the kittens for a day or two. If you pick them up during that time, the mother refuses to feed them, or else eats them. That's something we've always known about animals. It's humans we know very little about, or are only just starting to learn. Nobody ever put me on my mother's belly and left me there, still wet from my birth. What they did with me was wash me, wrap me in a pretty bundle, and put me in a cradle next to the big bed.

I don't have any memory of childhood, any memory of bodies from my childhood, either mine or my mother's. I construct a memory out of men's bodies, belatedly save myself with men's bodies, as an adult I invent a childhood, wet from the sperm that gave me birth.

There was one whole day when I was saturated with the thing, when it clung to my skin. As if I'd never left that short-stay hotel, or its sickly smell, or the crumpled sheets pulled up so that the bare mattress showed through. But I didn't try to rid myself of it. I didn't even look at my body. I stayed at home the whole day, huddled up in bed. From time to time, a little blood ran between my legs. When evening came, I stripped off and looked at myself in the mirror.

Gilles rang the bell while I was looking at myself in the mirror. I had no idea he was coming. He came out of the blue, at a crucial moment when what happened could either have become fixed or disappeared. When his gaze rested on my naked body, the whole thing became real. I wish I could extract the essence of that gaze, drink it in little sips, or lay it between my breasts, absorb it like a perfume, knowing it's something I'll never have, that straightforward way of looking at things, so sober and inscrutable, so fair in its judgment that you just have to respond immediately and with total sincerity.

I remember his toneless voice. "What happened?"

And I see my body again as it appeared to me in the mirror—bruises on the crotch, wide red streaks on the thighs and buttocks, and on the belly too, close to the pubic hair, and those two distinct cuts, one on the right breast, the other to the left of the navel.

"Something stupid," I replied.

And for a time, the memory was labeled "stupid"—the time it took Gilles to get used to it. Then he undressed, sat down on the edge of the bed, and began to touch me. He did it very gently, until I greeted the orgasm by stretching my arms and legs and crying out, as usual. When everything was calm again, he touched me very lightly in the places where I had been hit, like a doctor examining a patient.

"Do you want to talk about it?"

So I said, in a solemn voice, that naked, defenseless voice that coming always releases in me:

"I answered an ad."

The truth is, I answered a dream. One night I dreamed that an unknown man took me by force, with grim determination, his gestures so precise and quick he could as easily have been murdering me as making love to me. Above our two bodies, two birds were flying. One was a peacock, his tail spread in a helix, flying the way no peacock has ever flown, graceful as a swan and strong as an eagle. The other was a bird-woman with blood-red feathers. She spiraled to the ground, crash-landed, and lay there in her scarlet finery. I recognized myself in her, I was that winged woman, it was my face that looked up at the sky while my body surrendered to the stranger's violent lovemaking. Beside us, an open box, containing an assortment of instruments—pliers, tongs, scalpels. I looked at them, surprised and deeply curious. Who was going to open me up, and why? I trembled with desire, the desire to be at the mercy of tools like those, which cut through flesh, pull the wounds open, and keep them open.

I never read the paper with the classified ads, I never buy it. I read the daily papers. Not the stuff about politics. The kinds of things I read are crime reports, stories about rapes, or else film and theater reviews, interviews with actors. I admire judges and film directors, but I think actors, like criminals and their victims, are worthy of the brightest and most unequivocal thing I have in me—fascination.

It was Gilles who gave me the paper with the classified ads, because I was worried about what would happen to the kittens after they were born—I didn't want to put any of them to sleep, I wanted them all to live. In the paper, you can offer kittens to give away, everyone does it. There are several sections: "houses, apartments, furniture, cars, animals . . ." A pity they don't have a section for "babies," babies to give away, so you can choose one, just like that, and take it home with you in a Moses basket bought specially, all in pink gingham, a surprise for the man you love, even if he's not your man and never will be.

Usually, after "animals" come the personals. And there was the ad. It wasn't the only one, there were thirty at least, but that's the one I saw, straightaway, because it matched the dream, gave off the same vibrations, as if it had a magnet hidden in it and my pupils had turned into iron filings.

"Masterful man seeks flexible young woman to share intimate moments . . ." There followed a post office box and the name of a town, my town, the town where I worked, where I loved, with its black canal under an open sky and its motionless barges, the very town where I live.

I can still see myself sitting at the kitchen table, writing, I can still see myself throwing the letter in the nearest box, the one at the corner of the avenue. It must have been ten in the evening, and the air smelled of vanilla, or more likely lime trees in blossom. The neon signs of the restaurant floated in the black water of the canal. People passed, chatting, and on the café terrace a guitarist was passing a hat around. It might have been the south of France, or a secluded cove in a Greek port, a cove where boats don't go, only people strolling idly up and down the quays. I thought of the customers at the agency. They're always on the lookout for unusual destinations, and I try my best to satisfy them, because it's my job. My way of changing scenery is to answer an ad, with the night air starting to smell of vanilla and the cool dirty waters of the canal stirring memories of vacations.

"I couldn't help myself . . . Do you understand?"

"No," Gilles said.

He lit a cigarette and took a drag, screwing up his eyes. When he opened them again, the circles of his lashes were like two stars.

"It was bound to happen. I should have known one day you'd do the dirty on me."

That gentle voice of his, absorbing the catastrophe at the speed of light. Gilles always wins, even when he loses.

I laughed. "As long as I don't give you a baby—"

Gilles stood up abruptly, leaving us, the bed and me, in disarray. You don't give a baby to a man who's married with kids, you make do with crumbs, gaps in the schedule, improvised lovemaking at the end of the day, and you take your pill every morning, because you're a big girl and you have a sense of responsibility.

But all I want, sometimes, is a baby, and for everything else to disappear. A baby in my belly, and then in my arms, like my sister. My sister has a baby already, and she'll have more, she's the kind of woman who lives through her belly—the belly that makes babies, not the one you give your lovers.

Once I'd mailed my reply, the world seemed to shake around me, tiny cracks spreading rapidly like ripples across a calm surface. The very next day, a stranger would have my name, my address, my telephone number, the suggestion we meet in a local bar, a little bit of information about me—height, weight, hair color, details of what I'd be wearing so he could spot me easily. He would have the power to confirm the appointment or not, to turn up or to stay away, to station himself under my windows and watch me coming out every morning and follow me to the travel agency, or else approach me and see a smile form on my face . . . I had started to smile at passersby, as if every man I met could be the stranger. It was a vague smile, ambiguous—I might have been smiling because of the fine weather, or because everyone on the street was wearing flannel and cotton, but I could just as easily have been smiling like a woman in love, because of some secret that only I knew. I did have a secret—the dream. I knew nothing about the man in the ad, but the dream had inflamed me, I was excited and afraid at the same time, as if approaching a ritual. Waiting for the appointed day, I was like a disciple preparing, bending my neck in imagination, kissing the hand of the Master and the attributes of his office—pliers, tongs, scalpel.

But when the day came and I saw the man—he had confirmed nothing, leaving me in suspense up until the last minute—when he stood up and walked toward me in the bar I had indicated in my letter, he seemed so nondescript, I found him quite ugly. He didn't shake my hand. I couldn't read anything in his eyes as he looked me over, except perhaps a touch of annoyance, as if my red scarf—the color I had indicated—was excessive, my makeup artificial, my perfume obvious.

We sat down on the terrace. He ordered a coffee and I asked for an iced tea. He started to talk, mopping his forehead with a paper handkerchief. For a moment I thought he was going to say he had been sent by his Master, the way it happens in the stories. He certainly gave no impression that he found me attractive, or even that he was looking at my body with any thought of what he would do to it. In fact, he seemed completely uninterested in me. All he did was talk, on and on, as if to reassure himself. I listened to him, dumbstruck, thinking about the ways I could refuse, preparing them, polishing them. I looked at his narrow shoulders, his slightly stooped back, his very short hair, blond verging on red, his freckled skin, very white on the arms, red on the face because of the sun that day, and his eyes squinting under the light. I thought of what I would tell Gilles. "You know, I answered an ad, just to see, and when I saw the guy, I realized—" I would describe the man to him, making fun of him, just one more little massacre among thousands of others on the planet, like squashing a mosquito, nothing more. Then I would stroke Gilles's thick iron-gray hair and run my finger over his long lashes, and I would ask him to touch me lightly between my shoulder blades, in the sensitive spot we discovered by chance while making love, and in other places too, everywhere, with those long supple fingers of his that travel over my body with the boldness and gentleness of a beautiful language.

"I have a boyfriend," I told the guy.

He didn't look at me. He seemed worried.

"That's a drag. I don't want any problems with your boyfriend."

He gulped his coffee, took the cookie from his saucer, unwrapped it, and gave it to me. "What are you looking for, exactly?" he asked through thin lips.

"I don't know."

I finished my tea, then ate the cookie, saying, "Thank you very much," like a schoolgirl. The sun was burning hot, the terrace packed. It seemed to me the man was constantly asking the same question, with the addition of a few crude words, almost like a doctor probing for symptoms.

"What is it you like? Every woman's different. How about fellatio? Or sodomy? Some like it, some don't."

I felt tremendously weary. "I don't mind it," I said. "I don't mind anything."

Just then, I remembered the dream. I felt numb.

"As long as I'm dominated," I murmured, "I'll do anything."

We arranged to meet the following week.

NIGHT IN THE AFTERNOON

The next day and the days after that, I worked as usual, ate, slept, shopped, went about my business, saw Gilles occasionally. But all that time, I was waiting. While I slept, while I ate, while I talked to customers, while I kissed Gilles gently on the lips, I was waiting. I was cool, self-possessed, a victim of a condition that is very familiar to me, the total freezing of my emotions. It's a chronic disease, inherited from childhood, imprinted in the genes of well-to-do families, masters of their possessions and their affections. Nothing in my life gives me any motivation to break free of the condition, except dreams, those subtle combinations of vivid images that somehow conspire to save me. According to what they tell me, I form attachments or break them.

The red-headed man had suggested we go by train. The hotel where he wanted to take me was in the city, and you could never find anywhere to park. I arrived at the station five minutes before the train left. He was waiting for me under the clock, looking anxious.

"I didn't think you'd come."

He was more familiar than before. More worried too. I wondered why he didn't have a suitcase or an overnight bag with him. Where did he keep his whips and chains? If I couldn't be attracted to a Master—I'd abandoned that idea the first moment I met him—at least I wanted a ritual, symbolic objects, I wanted blindfolds, rope to bind my wrists, whips of different sizes, dildos, harnesses, leather collars. The lack of accessories revolted me. But I didn't let anything show, and I didn't ask any questions. We got our tickets

13

and went onto the platform, and I continued to be very formal with him.

It was a suburban station, a quiet station with only two tracks. There were red roses on the walls, and a black cat running into a tunnel covered with graffiti, naive and crude but fairly mild suburban graffiti. There were also two black women in bright dresses, standing on different platforms and shouting across the tracks. They were telling each other a story we didn't understand, and laughing, with easy, uncontrolled laughter, African laughter. While we waited for the train, the red-headed man took out some mail from the pocket of his light leather jacket and opened it. A pornographic magazine, some publicity for the Erotica Show, and a letter. He skimmed through the letter and handed it to me.

"Read it."

"It's not addressed to me."

"Read it."

I read quickly, in a fog. It was a woman like me, answering his ad. She had watched S/M videos, and liked what she saw, but she was afraid. Did he do things like that— whip women till the blood ran, hang them by their breasts, sew up their labia? Would she be branded, sodomized with different-sized objects, gang-banged? I looked up. The man was watching me.

"I don't reply to women who are afraid," he said.

"I'm not afraid," I said, watching the cat move along the wall with the red roses. In the silence, the black women laughed. Everything could stay like this, forever.

★ ★ ★

NIGHT IN THE AFTERNOON

By the time we got off the train, the city was like an oven. It was too early, the room was booked for three o'clock, we had half an hour to kill. We walked until we found a café. As the red-headed man pushed open the door, something fell to the tiled floor with a slight noise. It was a bright pink plastic clothespin. The man bent down, picked it up, and stuffed it in his pocket. Where had it come from, and why was he so anxious to retrieve it? It was a mystery, and because of it, one of those slight shifts took place in my mind, the kind that take you into another world, where the faces look like paintings and the tables and chairs like film sets, so that everything is suddenly like a fiction, and life is transfigured by something as small as a pink clothespin falling on a tiled floor.

We ordered two coffees. For some reason, I had the idea it wasn't the right time of day to ask for a glass of wine, and for a moment that trivial detail became the focus of all my anxieties. All the same, I needed a drink.

"I think I'd prefer a little wine," I told him shyly, feeling I was blaspheming.

Without hesitation, the man stood up, went to the counter, and changed my order. He came back and sat down. We said nothing until the coffee and the wine arrived. The waitress was middle-aged, strong and brown-skinned, her hair tied in a loose bun. She was wearing a white apron over a black dress. It would have seemed old-fashioned anywhere else in the city, but here, in this area of offices and ministries, it seemed just right. All she needed was white gloves, and she'd look the way maids used to in the old days.

CAROLINE LAMARCHE

The red-headed man and I started to talk. We seemed to have been saying exactly the same words over and over since we first met. I told him again that I needed to be dominated, that I'd do anything as long as I was dominated. He showed me the magazine he'd received that morning, a touch apologetically, it seemed to me. It wasn't up to much, he said, it was commercial, he didn't know why they still sent it to him, he didn't ask for it. I leafed through it. There were photos of naked women with shaved pubises sitting on bottles or masturbating themselves with their fingers, their nails enormously long. There were women licking men's cocks, and women with brooches in their breasts, dog collars around their necks and whips in their hands. Some of the women wore figure-hugging leather suits that covered them from head to toe, their faces masked, with only a slit for their eyes and a circle for their mouths. In these outfits, they either stood in dominating poses or lay with their legs apart on leather gynecological seats with stirrups for the feet and straps to hold the limbs in place. The photos were mediocre, revolting in their banality. I told him so, adding that it was a pity, an artist like Mapplethorpe could have done something marvelous with a subject like that, and I repeated "marvelous," but I was thinking of Mapplethorpe's flowers, because I hated all the rest, all those nudes of Mapplethorpe's that meant so much to people who treat sex as some kind of bodybuilding exercise. The tulips and orchids, though—from the front or the side, open or closed, they were so perfect they made you want to cry, they were marvelous, that was the only word you could use. The man agreed, though he seemed a bit embarrassed. Maybe he'd never heard of Mapplethorpe.

I turned a few pages and came to the ads.

"Obviously, there's something for every taste," he said, a trifle shamefaced, as if he was personally to blame for the advertisers' whims.

I had to read slowly to try to decipher the abbreviations and the specialized terms. I asked him to explain about certain practices—fetishism, for example, or the use of women as maids at high-class evening parties, or the stretching of the labia to eight centimeters, attached with elastic bands to the thighs under a miniskirt.

"It's ridiculous," I said, and forced myself to laugh heartily, like a playground supervisor trying to share the children's jokes.

Yes, he muttered, it was ridiculous, that was why he never advertised there. He placed his ads in the Saturday paper, and he made them discreet, just enough so that a woman interested in things like that would understand. I looked up and stared at his pale eyebrows and, with sudden intensity, recited from memory: "Masterful man seeks flexible young woman to share—"

He interrupted me, not at all aggressively, and explained patiently that two or three years ago, even such a mild ad would have been censored by the paper and returned to the sender. Today you could write that sort of thing if you were careful. "Flexible" was more acceptable than "submissive," for example, and anyway, "flexible"—he hesitated—"looks better." As he spoke, he shot me a somber and almost vindictive look. Our eyes met. I started to leaf through the magazine again, mechanically.

"I'm very flexible," I said, my eyes lowered. "I can touch my toes with my fingers."

"The people who are interested in these things," he said, "go a lot further than that."

An uneasy silence fell, filled for him, I guess, with visions that went "a lot further." The phrase amused me. I was starting to find the man interesting. Without intending to, he was demonstrating the huge gap between us. There was something quite ridiculous about the two of us together. We were so different, we seemed like grotesque caricatures to each other. A well-bred doll who never went "a lot further" and a bad guy who couldn't be taken seriously, each twinkling like a star in its own sky, light years from the other—me with my dreams of birds, him with his weird questions. Would I like to be dominated by several men, for example? I just had to say the word. There were plenty of people interested, the main difficulty was finding a day and a time that suited everybody.

"You have to realize, life isn't like in the books, where people arrange to meet in dungeons with all the right equipment. In life, you have your job from nine to five, your family from five to nine, apartment buildings are full of housewives and screaming brats, and ten of you can't all go up to a hotel room at the same time. But anyway, if you want to, I can try. How about it?"

He laughed, a feeble laugh that made me nauseous. I smiled. There was quite a long silence, filled with the noise his spoon made as he stirred his coffee.

"Anyway, I'm a stickler for hygiene. No penetration without a condom."

"Of course," I said, and thought of the men I'd known. None of them could stand the things.

"Around here," he added, "there are times during the day when the sewers are clogged with all the condoms coming down. Which just shows they're all at it—lawyers, doctors, government employees, all of them—all day, every day, but especially in the afternoons, in private houses, little hotels, that's all there is around here, all the streets are full of them, but you won't see anything, they all look anonymous from the outside."

I listened, fascinated. The city was a gigantic brothel.

"That's marvelous," I said.

"Marvelous" again. It was a word we used a lot when I was growing up, a very kind and tolerant word—a marvelously close family, a marvelous reception, a marvelous piece of charitable work, a certificate of excellence at school, that's marvelous, dear, marvelous.

He smiled rather distantly, without looking at me. It was nearly three o'clock, and the wine was going to my head. I asked him about his family, that's what you're supposed to do to put people at their ease when the conversation drops, it's what I was taught to do when I used to visit Margot in her old people's home. Margot, the last survivor of a generation of maids in black dresses and white aprons, Margot red-faced and wrinkled in her old age, like one of those varieties of apples they don't grow anymore. I was fifteen years old, fifteen years of comfort and breeding, with a pleated skirt over exquisite calves, and a kind smile, a perfectly sincere smile that hid a marvelous sadness, the sadness rich children feel when they discover that there's no way to cross the divide between their world and the world of those poorer than themselves, and that the whole universe will always be divided in two, till the end of time. Margot responded with good grace to my well-bred compassion, like someone speaking from one bank of a river to someone on the other bank, while contemplating the majestic river between them, an impassable border.

The red-headed man, though, replied with bad grace, and something of that old delicious sadness came back. His was a real hard-luck story—he was abandoned by his parents at birth. There really is such a thing as denial of paternity, it's even written in the parish registers for everyone to read, you just have to ask, he said insistently, as if anxious to convince me. The fact that it was down in black and white seemed to be what impressed him most. The rest followed naturally. Brought up in institutions. As a teenager, ran away from it all. Found a job as a messenger in the city, then as a waiter in a restaurant. Then this and that—little jobs. Twenty years of little jobs. He might have been talking about a twenty-year love affair, or a twenty-year career. A real loser, in other words, but a good guy all the same, the cream of the underprivileged, who hadn't joined the ranks of those who rape or kill because of their grim childhoods, the kind of men who get mentioned on the front pages of my favorite newspapers.

He repeated that he was free during the day, and that in the future we could see each other at whatever time suited me best.

"Abandoned at birth." Someone actually wrote that in black and white. In a register intended to record death as well as life, the kind of register that had recorded the births in my own family—"son of . . . , daughter of . . ."—branching out into a solid, well-respected tree, decorated with coats of arms.

"In the future," he'd said, and "whatever time suits you best." A man who didn't seem busy, who didn't slot me into the gaps in his day, a man abandoned by time. There were people all around us, businesspeople, a few workers with broad shoulders and solid trades, and there I was, sipping my glass of wine, and there was the man, so totally at my disposal I couldn't bear it, drinking his third cup of coffee and letting time pass.

"Well," I said, "it's after three. Are we going or not?"

"Why? Have you changed your mind?" He seemed unconcerned. "Do you want us to stay here and talk?"

It seemed to me we could easily do just that. But we fell silent again, and the effect of the wine was wearing off. We either had to say goodbye right now or let our bodies do the talking.

"If we're staying," I said, "I'll need more wine. If we're going, let's go quickly, I need to be a bit drunk like this to go."

21

He paid the bill and left a large tip. I never leave anything, I just pick up the change. A cup of coffee's expensive enough, for something you could just as easily drink at home.

"I didn't think people tipped anymore."

"I've been a waiter," he said simply. "I know what it means to get a tip."

I felt a new and unexpected emotion. Something like respect for him, and for people like him, the kind of people he defended when he said "keep the change." Shame, too, at having thought for so long that a nice smile was enough.

We went out. We turned onto one street among all the others. I looked at the sun-drenched housefronts.

"Don't try to look for it," he said. "You can't see anything from outside."

The house was tall and gray, with a nineteenth-century front and a solid door. We went in without ringing. Here we were, we'd arrived, it'd soon be over, this thing that would be just like the red-headed man—rather strange, rather sad, on the margins of other people's lives. Suddenly, I thought of Margot. Whenever I went to see her, I told myself the same thing: It'll soon be over. An hour in another world, and then straight back home—instant relief. I remember a big four-poster bed, just one, that took up a whole wall and a corner of the window. I remember a chair—maybe there were two, but Margot always sat on the bed when I came, and I sat on the chair, so there must have been just one. There was a washbasin somewhere, I can't remember where, and a wardrobe, I can't remember that either. I wonder if you saw those things when you were fifteen. I wonder what you saw, when you were fifteen. You saw people's bodies, Margot's very thick legs that seemed swollen with water, you heard her labored breathing, you remember she kept saying: "My emphysema." You saw her yellow complexion, her partially toothless smile that made her look like a witch, you breathed in the sickly smell, you heard the irritating ticking of the big red alarm clock, but you kept coming, bravely, every week, because the whole edifice—good deeds, love, the sense of life—had always rested on Margot. You came to hear Margot talk about her youth, the time she worked for your family as a maid, and how, whenever the trains were on strike, she would walk to work, two hours there, two hours back, following the railroad track because she didn't know the roads well, and besides, work is sacred, and you mustn't disappoint your employers. She'd had good legs in those days, but now they were heavy, not to mention the emphysema. You came because Margot asked you one day if you were going to marry and have children, and when you answered yes, of course, she told you in a low voice that if it hadn't been for the work and the employers' children, especially "you, dear, I pulled you out of this incredible jumble of sheets, you could have suffocated," if it hadn't been for all that, which added up to a kind of family life, she would have married. Yes, the opportunities were there, but first take care of those close to you, those closest to you—those who employ you and whom you end up loving—because in any case, men always manage, even with a broken heart. You came because Margot whispered that kind of thing as she looked through the half of the window that wasn't hidden by the bed. You came because there was a broken heart, a belly as dry as a pod on legs that were too thick, and it was fascinating that Margot could laugh, despite everything, and love you so much that one day she gave you her bracelet of imitation pearls and imitation stones, in a setting of imitation gold. You ran errands for her, fetched her cotton balls, aspirin, a battery for her flashlight, and you brought her flowers from Mama's garden, flowers the gardener had grown, flowers that didn't cost anything. You brought cakes you'd made yourself, you were good at making cakes, but only cakes, because for everything else there was the cook to do it, that was why you didn't know how to make coffee or fry eggs, but cakes, yes, you invited your girlfriends over on Saturday afternoons to make cakes, and on Sundays, after Mass, you went to see Margot and had coffee and cake. And then when you started college, far enough away so you didn't have to come back every week, you said goodbye to Margot, thinking you'd see her in a year, and two months later, Margot died, and some time after that, you received in the mail a little package of her last treasures—the red alarm clock, a statuette of Our Lady of Lourdes, a boxwood rosary—along with a note from the lawyer saying she'd put it in writing that she wanted you to have these things. It was all so sad and so typical and proved how useful love was—it must have been love that prolonged the old woman's life through all those visits. And maybe you should give yourself to the red-headed man in the same way, only here there was an added sense of the ridiculous, how ridiculous it was going to be, fucking in a short-stay hotel, and how disgusting, because here there was no love, and certainly no death.

A little entrance hall. A staircase. To the left of the staircase, a door with a window, leading to an office. The door was closed, and there was a note stuck behind the handle: "I'm at the grocer's. Indicate the room you're using and the time you arrived." Followed by room numbers from one to ten, with little circles that had to be blacked in. They all had been, except for number seven.

"I'll go have a look at the room," the red-headed man said.

He ran upstairs. I stayed where I was, leaning against the front door. And then the door opened, pinning me against the wall, and the manager came in. She looked me up and down. She must have been beautiful once, and maybe she still was. I find it hard to judge that kind of tired, rather casual beauty. The red-headed man came back down.

"I've been up to see room seven. Apparently it's the only one free."

The woman looked at the paper with the circles. "That's right, number seven. You can have it."

I thanked her and smiled, quite boldly. I wanted her to see it meant nothing for me to come here, it was no different from going somewhere to have a drink or see a show, there was nothing special about this place, it was just an ordinary house, and I was just a weary traveler, a guest being shown to her room for an afternoon nap.

"Two hours," the woman said. "Two hours and that's it. Any more and it's extra."

We went upstairs. Our room was on the second floor. There were other doors, all closed. The house was completely silent, as if all the rooms were empty, or as if everyone really did come here to sleep or to listen in silence to what was happening in the other rooms—what was about to happen in room seven, for instance, where the red-headed man was stepping aside now for me to enter.

A big room, a big bed covered with a purple spread, high windows with thick curtains, drawn so tightly that not a speck of sunlight filtered into the room, and in a corner, a washbasin and a bidet concealed behind another curtain. I looked around, not knowing what to do.

"It's very nice."

"Do you think so?"

It looked as if he was going to start his endless chatter again, so very quickly I said, "Yes, not bad at all," and walked around, pretending to be interested in the prints of naked women in languid poses. But all the while I was thinking: He won't be able to stop talking, I'll have to keep putting him at his ease, he'll just grope me halfheartedly and it'll be awful, really awful.

"What now?"

"Get undressed."

I didn't move. I was expecting him to talk, expecting the same weary litany, the same vague and repetitive words, the same clumsy excuses.

He said nothing.

NIGHT IN THE AFTERNOON

I turned my back on him and started taking off my dress. He'll see now, I thought, he'll see I've put on my best set of underwear—dark red lace as fine and shiny as silk, a half-cup bra to give extra uplift to the breasts—and he won't be able to resist, he'll undress me himself, the way Gilles does, sometimes gently, sometimes feverishly, depending on his mood, his hands will caress me through the material, eager to touch me, moving under my arms, around my breasts, slipping off the straps.

But nothing happened. He didn't say a word. He didn't compliment me on what I was wearing. And when at last I was naked, he still said nothing. I could feel him looking at me, but he didn't seem the least bit aroused, he was looking at me with the eyes of a doctor or a horse dealer, coldly measuring and evaluating, concerned only with surfaces, the texture of the skin, the curve of the back.

"On your knees!"

I knelt by the bed. I used to kneel by the bed to say my prayers when I was a child. Margot used to kneel too, on her swollen knees. She was the one who taught me the words of the prayer. Thank you. Forgive me.

The man grabbed the back of my neck, forced my chest down onto the bed and then let go. Next, he placed his hands on my buttocks and started to knead them the way I used to knead dough for those fruitcakes Margot loved so much, that was how the man took the measure of my flesh, rapidly, with the flat of his hands, then suddenly he thrust his fingers into me, like a cook mixing currants or cherries with dough, or hiding a charm in the middle of a Twelfth Night cake.

"Lie down."

I got up on the bed and lay on my stomach.

"Spread your legs."

The orders were coming faster now.

"More."

He grabbed my thighs and pulled them wide apart, then left me in that position.

There was a noise of paper being crumpled angrily, and in the expectant silence of the room, the sudden noise filled me with terror. The man slipped his hands under me and groped for my breasts. He kneaded them, went away, returned, and placed two pins on them. A sharp pain flooded me from my nipples to my armpits. I bit my wrists to stop myself from crying out and raised myself on my elbows, holding my breath. The man pushed me back down on the bed, squashing my chest onto the pins. They were plastic clothespins, just like the one that had fallen on the tiled floor of the café a little while before. My dream of metal brooches with chains and weights attached and all sorts of jewels puncturing my chest—that dream evaporated. I was the clothespin woman.

Again the noise of rustling paper, a noise that drove me crazy. I knew what it was now. The man had a bag with him, a bag full of things. He must have been hiding it under his leather jacket. And now he was getting ready to take something else out.

With quick, skillful movements, he tied a scarf over my eyes. Then I heard a purring sound, and suddenly the thing was inside me, it didn't seem especially large, but the man pushed it deep inside then pulled it out, more paper noises, and there was something else inside me, something bigger this time, which moved and hummed. I was breathing hard, my hands clutching at the sheets, searching desperately for something to hold on to. The thing came out, more rustling of paper, then the man was on top of me, crossing my wrists and winding a rope around them three times and pulling it very tight, all with the same rapid and precise movements. I could feel something new at the entrance to my vagina, something that didn't move or make a noise, he rammed it in brutally and it dilated me, swelled inside me, it was stiff and yet flexible, he pushed it in deeper, deeper still, I felt as if I was going to explode, I lifted my chest in panic, but he just kept punching it into me like a maniac, my belly was a bell and this monstrous clapper kept striking against it, I could feel my vagina now against the abdominal wall, as if the thing was going to burst through my skin near the navel, I never imagined it was possible to go so far, so high, in such an unheard-of direction, the thing kept right on, relentlessly, as if it had a life of its own, and at last I let myself go and cried out, I cried that I was afraid, afraid, afraid, my vagina was on fire, my mucous membranes consumed by the flames, the clapper and the bell had become one inside me, tolling with the urgency of an alarm, soon it would be too late, the entire landscape would be razed to the ground, laid waste forever. In a last violent reflex of survival, at the limits of pain and exhaustion, my muscles rebelled, my knees lifted, my back arched, I wriggled like an eel, and the thing slipped out and landed against my thigh, still twitching uselessly.

CAROLINE LAMARCHE

For a fraction of a second, there was silence. An eternity, punctuated by the sharp pain in my breasts and the fire in my belly. The paper noise started up again, and my skull echoed with rustlings that seemed to emerge from the walls and the ceiling, making the room a huge echo chamber. In my struggle, the blindfold had moved, and I could see an area of wallpaper with a gold filigree pattern, then the man jumping naked onto the bed, his torso narrow and sweating. I didn't know when he'd undressed, or why, but he'd kept his socks on, gray woollen socks like the ones maids used to knit, and I felt disgusted, I imagined he must have warts or deformed feet. In a flash, I remembered my own wart, a little whitish circle, healed now. I had all the hours I spent at the swimming pool to thank for it. I got salicylic acid from the drugstore, and day after day I'd put it on and watch the imperfection burn, watch the skin get whiter and shrivel and become painful. For a while, it looked as if the root infection would spread to the whole foot, and I wouldn't be able to walk anymore. I'd scratch it and rub it with lime and put the acid on again, over a period of weeks. And I'd make love with Gilles with my feet stuck to the bed so that he shouldn't notice anything. Ridiculous. Ridiculous that love should be tainted by such reflexes, that there was always a wart somewhere, always litter lying about in the most beautiful landscape, always Japanese tourists in front of the *Mona Lisa*. The only love that wasn't ridiculous was chaste love, the love of maids—Margot, where are you, see what the world is coming to, what my thoughts have come to—I'm looking at the gray socks of a man who's torturing me, and thinking of my wart.

I closed my eyes, determined to keep them closed. The pain in my breasts was fading, the pins were still there but there was no longer anything squashing them, and now my wrists were being untied and my arms spread wide on the bed. Then a strap landed on my belly and my thighs. My skin became inflamed in patches, up to the edge of the pubic hair, and it was clear the man knew what he was doing, going around the sensitive area like that, demarcating it, in a way, while leaving it intact, striking just at the border—my cunt was like a top that he was spinning around faster and faster with every blow. The man struck savagely but methodically, without uttering a word, and I didn't cry out, but my whole body jumped as if it had a life of its own, unrestrained by my mind, unaffected by fear or anger. I felt no emotion, I let my body do all the work, let it jump and fall back. My arms, my head, and my knees were against my chest now, as if I wanted to enter myself, become my own fetus, but I didn't want anything, anything at all, it was the body that wanted, it was the body that left only the back exposed, like a snail its shell. Untroubled by my change of position, the man continued striking my back with his invisible strap. He himself was invisible, even in my mind. The one-dimensional image I had of him, from before he pushed me onto the bed, bore no relation at all to my perception of the man who was bending me double with these stinging blows. It couldn't be the same man—no normal person could believe that. The distance was too great. This man could kill me.

"Open!" he cried. But I couldn't, my whole body refused. The man stopped hitting me. Calmly, he unfolded me, opening my legs and my arms with such authority that I just lay there in a crucified position. I thought he was going to kill me, and I waited to feel his hand on my throat. But it was something else that came and brushed against my lips.

"Suck! Suck!" he cried. My brain felt empty. I began to suck his latex-clad cock. He placed his hand flat on my skull and tipped my head up toward him, forcing it to move backward and forward, as if I were a doll with a movable neck. His protected cock was just one more thing, he touched me only with things. I wanted to touch his naked skin. I tried, grasping his wrist and squeezing it so hard, I could have broken it.

But he misunderstood. "You like it, don't you? Anyone would think you've been doing it all your life."

I spat out his cock. I felt nauseous.

"Go tell that to my *boyfriend*!" I cried.

I thrust the word "boyfriend" at him like a shield, a lance, a war cry. My boyfriend, my lover, my treasure, my deep wound, the wound that makes me limp, that bites my heels, the tenacious wart I squash beneath my foot when I make love and burn maliciously, day after day, creating a mess, a massacre. It takes time to find your new skin, my angel. To carry the fire into the wound. To burn the sickness of love to the root.

"Sure I'll tell him," the man said calmly. "I'll tell him you're the biggest slut I've ever buggered, the whoriest whore of them all." Suddenly he yelled: "Say sorry, slut!"

Now. Now he was going to kill me. I wasn't a real slut. I'd never be one, however hard I tried. It was too far from me, as inaccessible as Margot's pure soul. That was why I deserved to die. I cried out I was sorry, sorry I wasn't a slut, sorry I'd never been able to see things right through to the end, had never gone to the end of anything, sorry that degradation was no more within my reach than beauty was. I said sorry, I cried that it was ridiculous, I was ridiculous, and I doubled up, mowed down by a volley of tears like gunshots, a dismembered puppet who would soon be on the front pages of the papers, the latest victim of the red-headed man, the red-headed man has struck again . . .

He didn't kill me. He was silent for a moment, without moving, as if my words had thrown him. I took advantage of the pause to bend my legs again and hold them tight to my belly. I didn't want anything more on my breasts, anything more in my vagina, I was protecting myself like an animal, my exhaustion at last complete.

"Calm down," the man said.

I unclenched my fists and my legs went limp. All he had to do now was unfold me and stretch me out and take off the pins, which he did. Immediately, the relaxation spread from the liberated area to the rest of my body. The absence of pain was an infinite pleasure. The man knelt and began to massage my breasts, then my belly, quickly but gently. There was no love in what he was doing, not even compassion, he was simply putting me back in working order, like a worn-out machine. He did it for a while, then lay down next to me. I was breathing weakly. I felt numb. From a long way away, I heard a final order:

"Don't fall asleep!"

His voice was dry. Maybe he would kill me if I fell asleep. Maybe he had to control himself not to go as far as that—his hands on my neck, pulling the scarf tighter and tighter. I licked his side, like an animal. His skin was smooth and incredibly soft, bathed in sweat. My tongue moved, working like a terrified animal, to arouse him—it was the only way to survive. The man didn't flinch. So I continued, my eyes closed, licking higher, as far as the nipples, then down to the groin. I opened my eyes and saw his blond pubic hair against his cock, and ate his blond hair, my mouth full of it, and licked his cock. He took off the condom and let me go ahead. He was like a kitten with its mother. I licked him the way a mother cat licks its young, with application. He was weak now, he could have been my child, perhaps I was giving birth to him at that very moment. He didn't know it, not yet, and began to speak in a toneless voice:

"I don't get a hard-on easily."

He said it straight out, without hesitation, just like one of his orders.

"It doesn't matter," I replied, my mouth against his cock. "I can do this for hours."

I thought it and set about it. My whole being was devoted to that one thing—getting him to come, if possible. It was a kind of compassion, but it didn't come from me. It was some-thing I learned from Gilles, who's often talked about it—how he's concerned only for my pleasure, how he puts himself second, ready to tire himself out to make me come. At that moment I was transmitting to the red-headed man a skill that wasn't mine. But maybe it's always like this—you're the ser-vant of your lover, and you shouldn't expect anything in return but the assurance that the gift will be passed on to some-one else, another child, whether virile or impotent.

The red-headed man didn't say if he liked it. Maybe he didn't feel anything. He touched my hair with his hand, very lightly, like a breath, and I knew that he was no longer in command. Those trembling fingers, that directionless ges-ture, told me that his body was separating from his will, surrendering to a nameless sweetness. It took a long time for him to come, a very long time, and when he felt that he was almost there—his cock, in my mouth, started to tremble with an independent life that I found strangely moving—the man pulled himself away from me, leaving me empty, and straightened up. I opened my eyes and saw him on his knees in front of me, his face closed and hard, and down below, his hand jiggling his cock mechanically with a kind of objectless hatred.

"I'm going to come over you."

And that's what he did, like when you pee on the grass, straight in front of you, and watch the grass shrivel and go yellow, stung by the acid water, that's the way he came over me, and I felt the hot drops hit me and slide down my face and stick to my eyelids.

"I can't see."

He took a corner of the sheet and wiped my eyes.

"Say thank you!"

I said thank you, and repeated it in an exhausted voice, like a beloved name. It was such a relief to say the words that I forgot to cry out, to feel nauseous, forgot I wanted to kill him.

Thank you. I say it today. Or rather, everything says it for me. Because I went through with it. I didn't shy away. So many people don't go through with it. I did, and the whole world is crying out its gratitude. It's midday, I'm walking home from the travel agency, along the boulevard. The kittens were born four days ago, I've been bleeding for five days, and for the first time I can feel the light and the shade, the coolness of the trees and the mildness of the air, on my skin. Before, everything stopped at my eyes. Now my whole body is open, and calm waves ripple through it. I must be smiling at the people I pass, or walking with a light but confident step, to judge by the looks I get, gentle looks, pleasantly surprised looks. So much gentleness, combined with the sharpness of my sensations, makes me want to die. Everything is in everything, the trees are in me and I'm in the serene faces of the passersby, and in the more enigmatic faces of the pigeons, the dogs, and the children. A subtle choreography regulates the smallest details. For once, everything has its place and its role in the dance, without encroaching on its neighbors. Even the cars glide on a cushion of air, the squealing of brakes and honking of horns seem to be thrown into the aural tapestry like a shower of toffees on a birthday. Everything is borne along on a single wave, and I carry the wave inside me as I walk, as if pregnant with it, my body marked with blows, swollen like a fresh bud. I carry life, that voracious creature, in the very places where I was hit—on the belly, on the cheeks—and men look at me as if I'm twenty, and the trees greet me with great impassioned gestures, and the wind swells me like a sail, I am a ship thrusting forward in a big beautiful storm.

I come back to the apartment and find Douce suckling her kittens. I stay and watch them. For a long time. Then Gilles phones, and his voice reaches not only my ears and part of my brain, but also the secret spot, the sensitive triangle between my shoulder blades.

"Hi, darling. How are you?"

I feel like kissing the receiver, eating the sound of that voice that will never abandon me, that will keep coming back for news of my breasts and belly and blood.

"I'm fine."

Then he asks me a question that takes me by surprise: "Tell me, when you were with that guy, what exactly were you looking for?"

"I wanted to cry," I answer, very quickly. "Just that, to cry."

"And did you cry?"

I barely hesitate. "No. I didn't come, I didn't cry. Nothing happened."

"Nothing?" Gilles says. "Nothing?" He laughs triumphantly, reducing my stupid gratitude to ashes. "All you managed to do was make yourself dirty and ridiculous!"

Well, at least that's something new, I tell myself—and I feel my flesh suddenly cracking up, reduced to sharp little pieces of ice—there hasn't been enough between you and me that was ridiculous, my darling, nor anything dirty either. There's been only beauty, that fucking beauty of love, something like the *Mona Lisa*'s smile behind bullet-proof glass, worn out by the flashes of the cameras, that fucking vision, that vision you're obliged to see, you've seen it, like you've seen everything, you don't even know what you were looking for any more.

"OK, I agree. It was dirty and ridiculous. But listen to me, Gilles, listen carefully—I did it once, and now it's over."

That's really what I think. It's what I was thinking on the journey back, in the train. I looked out at the landscape, the peeling back walls of suburban buildings, embankments invaded by wild grass and the kind of shrubs you don't see anywhere else, savage, neglected, abnormally vigorous. I remember monstrous plants, with whitish corollas—I thought they were hemlock. "Giant hogweed," the red-headed man corrected. That got him talking about his vegetable garden, the rhubarb that grew there in profusion—if I wanted, he could cut me a few stems—and the animals he looked after whenever the neighbors went on vacation, three dogs, a rabbit, and a canary. I told him Douce had given birth to three lovely kittens—did he want one? He laughed a bit without looking at me, saying that other people's dogs were enough for him, and the canary he let out from time to time to fly around the living room.

By the time we got off the train, the sun had faded from the wall with the red roses. The platform was deserted, the black cat nowhere to be seen. I noticed for the first time that there were two white lines running on either side of the track, and it struck me that they must continue like that, uninterrupted, all the way to the city, that someone must have painted them patiently for that specific purpose. It didn't cross my mind that they were there only to keep passengers from going too close to the edge of the platform. To me, they were there to lead you on, to hypnotize you into wanting to leave—even the train obeyed those white lines and not the tracks. I thought of Margot following the white lines on foot whenever there was a strike.

In front of the station, the man asked me if I wanted to see him again. I didn't know.

"I have a boyfriend," I repeated, indecisively.

But I was really thinking about the blood, questioning the burning between my legs. I would see what the blood said. If it stayed or if it went. Or if the wound became infected.

"It was very good," I said. "Really. But I don't know if I want to do it more than once."

His face was flat again, his eyes downcast, his smile weary.

"Answer the other women," I added. "Don't rely just on me."

He shrugged his shoulders. "I don't want to answer the other women now."

I told myself it was only natural. I was different from the other women who answer ads because I wasn't looking for anything. I'd simply had a dream, and chance had given me the illusion that I could make it come true. As for the rest, I didn't need anyone. Beauty, health, upbringing, affection—I had received more than the average woman. But that didn't mean I had to respond to the fantasies of every man who was abandoned at birth . . .

"Phone me on Monday."

What I was thinking was that it's easier to dump a guy over the phone.

The next day, Gilles arrived as I was looking at myself in the mirror. As I said before, he saw the marks on my body and made love to me.

I should mention that later, as I walked with him to his car, he started crying. It must have been eleven o'clock, maybe even midnight, the air smelled of the canal, the buses that passed on the street were empty.

"You could have lost me," Gilles said tragically, with his hand on the car door.

I could have sworn he had tears in his eyes, or at least in his voice. I don't mind that in a man, but just then they seemed out of place. I laughed.

"Lost you? Why?"

And then Gilles hit me, full in the face. I didn't cry out. "Thank you," I whispered, and buried my head in his shoulder. He wanted me desperately, he said, with a kind of terror, but we couldn't make love in the middle of the street, and besides, it was late, he had to get home to his wife and kids, and anyway, the blood between my legs put a stop to everything for the moment. So I told him I loved him, in a low, neutral voice, because I didn't want to shatter the hope I had—the hope that he would hit me again, the hope that he would replace the red-headed man—Gilles, with his beautiful eyes, his long lashes, his tall frame, and his cock that gets hard as soon as I brush against him.

2

The blood has stopped. The kittens' eyes are half open, though they're still sticky at the corners. I'm reminded of the red-headed man's sperm.

He phoned. "It's over," I said.

"Just knowing you exist," he said, "just knowing I could have a drink with you from time to time, would be enough for me."

"All right," I said. "I don't mind a drink."

I miss the blood. It was bright and very pure, quite unlike menstrual blood. The kind of blood you see in old paintings— Christ on the cross, the Virgin of the Seven Sorrows.

We have our drink on a café terrace. It's a fine day, the sky looks as if it's been given a thorough cleaning. I tell myself I'm not going to any more hotel rooms. Summer's coming, and I love the sun. I don't want to sacrifice any of my afternoons while the weather's fine. I'll work at the travel agency in the mornings, advising people who think that going away gives you a new lease on life, and then in the afternoons I can be alone in the woods, alone with Gilles. I tell myself the sun will help me say no.

I say yes. We're going to see each other again. Somewhere else. In another hotel. That way you'll be sure, the man says. I've said yes, and now I feel even more disgusted. But that's all to the good. My body will reject him in a way that my will never could. Once and for all.

At home, I've been watching Douce. Since the kittens started opening their eyes, she's been going out into the garden for longer periods, then coming back for a nap on my bed. She used to be submissive, now she's becoming dominant. I've seen her provoking the stray ginger tom who comes into the bedroom when my window's open and lolls shamelessly on the unmade bed. He lies there and watches Douce advance. They look each other up and down. He waits for her to beat a retreat, but she growls and throws herself on him. He runs off. She's surprised to see him go. Then she notices how rumpled the sheet is where they were fighting, and she crawls back in terror from the strange swelling in her resting place.

I put on a very short, figure-hugging dress. I'm too old for it, but that's the way it is. Things end, but you drink them to the last drop without understanding why.

Gilles arrives. He says I look beautiful, and I ought to take off everything I'm wearing underneath and be naked under the dress.

NIGHT IN THE AFTERNOON

★ ★ ★

Gilles takes me to the woods. We have two hours. As we stroll, we talk. About everything except the red-headed man. Neither of us wants to talk about him. It's not worth the bother.

Gilles smokes as he walks. I'm fascinated by the way he smokes, the way he screws up his eyes slightly. It makes him look gentle and hard at the same time. He's somewhere else, somewhere far from me. He walks away as he smokes, breathing in the whole world through the smoke, a world I'm temporarily excluded from. It's his respite from me. But for me it's another way to possess him, staring longingly at his beauty across the distance created by the cigarette. He has long hands, with well-groomed nails. When I think of his fingers, two images come to mind— a long, thin cigarette, and my swollen vulva.

He walks and smokes, and we talk. An hour goes by. I'm surprised he hasn't yet laid me down in the bracken. With an air of mystery, he turns and starts to walk back the way we came.

"Aren't you going to do anything to me?" I ask, but lightly, casually.

"Yes," he says. "Everything."

My belly becomes heavy, and I go weak at the knees. We walk on a little farther. Gilles points to a tree that's not like the others, a chestnut tree surrounded by beeches. I lean my back against it. Gilles lifts my dress and, with infinite gentleness, begins to touch me with his fingers.

"Your cunt is swelling like a fruit," he says. He's always impressed with that kind of natural display.

I can feel the fruit ripening, filling with juice at a dizzying rate, getting huge, oozing—what strange power my lover's hand has to bring such a flat, dry fruit to ripeness, to fill it in an instant with hot liquid and the desire to be picked or to explode under the exquisite pressure of his fingers. I explode. My knees give way against the trunk and my head goes back and the bark snags my hair, pulling it like a hand.

"You're a fast finisher," Gilles says.

My breath slows, stretches down to my feet. I straighten up, my back against the tree, my flesh melting into it, strengthened by the contact with this tree that is so different from the others, so sturdy and confident, strengthened, too, by my cry that ascended all the way up the trunk to the sky, to the thin clouds streaked by the topmost branches. I open Gilles's fly, plunge my hand inside his underpants, and take out his cock, which is already hard. Gilles gets a hard-on as soon as he touches me. Sometimes he gets one just by thinking about me when I'm not with him. It brings tears to his eyes—I know because he told me. Now, like a child, he puts himself in my power, letting my hands move back and forth, back and forth, and very soon I can sense he's about to come, so I undo the buttons that go up the front of my dress like a ladder and expose my naked and swollen belly and Gilles moans and comes over my skin. Looking down at the bright gel that covers my dark pubic hair, I laugh—it's so tepid and pure and milky inside, every time I move it quivers. When Gilles wipes me with the bracken, it's so sticky it won't go away, it's like the gel they put on your belly before an ultrasound, I remember going to the hospital with my sister when she was eight months pregnant, her skin stretched to breaking point, the male nurse applying the gel, then the probe gliding gently over her belly in a circular motion. I can still see the shape of the baby swimming on the screen, expanding like ectoplasm. You were supposed to marvel at the sight of an arm, a leg, a tiny cock, a heart beating regularly, but I couldn't make out anything, all I could see was moving life forms vaguer than dreams, than all my dreams of motherhood, indecipherable oceanic forms that bring tears to your eyes.

The spores of the bracken are sticking to my belly like gold dust, and Gilles tells me I'm the most beautiful woman in the world.

When I see the red-headed man again, when we're on the train going to the city, following the white lines on the platforms, he takes a quick look at me in my very short dress and tells me he wishes he were going out with a "real looker," so that passersby would turn around and envy him, but there are beautiful women who are nothing much in bed and others who . . . I don't resent what he's saying. I'm only surprised that Gilles thinks I'm so beautiful. Maybe this man's right, maybe it's time I realized I'll never be a "real looker."

The weather is glorious. On the embankments on either side of the railroad tracks, the giant hogweed sways like ivory umbrellas. I wonder why I'm going to shut myself away again behind closed curtains with this man. The one consolation is that it'll soon be over. But I feel as if I'm being unfaithful. To the sun, to the woods, to the free time that only Gilles can fill. I'm going to waste two hours of my life. A hole, a stain that will dirty the trees, the sky, and everything I've ever learned or ever will learn about love.

The red-headed man is talking without looking at me, staring down at the flap where I'm resting my elbow.

"I'd be happy to have what you don't give your boyfriend."

Without thinking, I protest that it's not like that. Everyone is unique, Margot used to say, you must have a thought for everyone when you say your prayers at night, and I repeat that everyone is unique, what I get from him is something Gilles can't offer—blows, unrestrained violence, violence without love, that more than anything, without love. It's so refreshing not to love, if you only knew—you do know, don't you?

Then I stop, taken aback, because he's looked up and I finally see him for what he is—a faithful dog, resigned to being abandoned again. His sadness is so absolute, I'm dazzled by it—it opens me more surely than any scalpel could, making me a bundle of exposed nerves and bared entrails, with my cunt quivering in the middle, a red gaping mouth open forever with the pain of the blows. I tell myself the red-headed man could be our dog, Gilles's and mine, he could be a dog that belongs to everyone, a dog that collects scraps from under the table.

"Are we there yet?" I ask, with a slight trembling in my voice.

We're nearly there, the man says, there are no more stops. And a great hole opens beneath me, and the vibration of the wheels penetrates me in a gentle and regular rhythm in time with the throbbing of my cunt. My body is preparing itself. I remember waking up last night, well before dawn, with the kind of feverish excitement you feel at the anticipation of sexual pleasure. But without pleasure, without any hope of it. Thinking only of the pain to come, like a poisonous shrub, a giant hogweed growing for some reason on a railroad embankment. I looked down at my pale body, the limbs stretching involuntarily, and the cunt I could no longer bring myself to touch, as if it carried death with it.

We're there. It's another hotel, a smaller one this time. An ordinary two-story, redbrick suburban house. There's a tall, well-built man perched on a ladder in the yard next door, cutting scrap metal with a blowtorch. He stops for a moment and turns to look at us, staring as we go around to the back door of the red house. I can feel his eyes on me, the eyes of a man cutting metal, a man with fire at the end of his arm, a dazzling fire you can't look at directly. I look down at the ground, pursued by his blinding gaze. He knows exactly why I'm wearing a short dress and how long it'll be before I come back out. I feel very weak suddenly, like molten metal being bent and shaped.

The red-headed man rings the doorbell. A little dog barks. The door is opened by a fat woman who leads us into an old-fashioned kitchen. She is in the middle of doing her ironing. Her linen is on the ironing board. The dog sniffs at my calves.

"The price includes a drink," the fat woman says. She's wearing an acid-green skirt and a spotted blouse.

We turn down the drink and go upstairs. The staircase is narrow and dark and echoes to our steps. The room is very small, almost an attic. There's a mattress on the floor, covered with a dark red bedspread. The gold floral wallpaper is peeling.

"Get undressed. Lie down."

I'm used to the orders by now—they're what I was made for. I lie on the mattress. The bedspread smells of other people, an indefinable mixture of secretions. I get up again and tear it off. Beneath it, the sheets are clean and cool to the touch. I have a strong desire to sleep.

"Spread your legs."

Shyly, I mention the blood and the bad night I had. The man says he'll be gentler this time. Maybe he's also been affected by the way the man next door looked at us, or troubled by the brightness of the blowtorch in the solar forge of the afternoon. Brightness on brightness. But inside the room, the curtains stifle the light and muffle cries, the darkness is pitiless.

The man doesn't put clothespins on my breasts or whip me. He penetrates me with his fingers and digs about inside. He asks me if my boyfriend has ever fucked me up the ass, and if so, how many times.

"Just once," I tell him, in a low voice, "and it hurt."

"Get down on all fours."

I do as he says.

"It's obvious you're not used to it," he says. "You need widening. Next time, we'll start with that."

There won't be a next time, you loser—that's what I'm thinking—you'll never see me again, me or my asshole. So go ahead, work on me all you want, one last time. That's what you do, methodically, with something I haven't had time to look at, something long and not too wide that forces an entry and then goes farther and deeper. I can feel it beating against the wall of the rectum, I get the impression it's going to burst through the wall into my vagina and come out the other side in a stream of blood and shit. It doesn't hurt. The only thing that hurts is the shame of being purged like a mare, I'm melting with shame and abandon, I'm afraid of what could come out when you remove your contraption, what could spurt in your face and spread across the bed and make the room stink, the room and the whole world, and make me a woman people either avoid or else spit at, closing their eyes and holding their noses. But my boyfriend, who's interested in everything, my boyfriend, my lover, he'll be next, loser, and he'll use the opening you're making. With his hard, gentle cock, he'll come and go, deep inside me, as far as he can, and he won't be afraid of causing me the pain I felt the first time.

I was the one who wanted it, one summer's day in the woods. I asked Gilles to kneel behind me, then I got down on all fours, spread my buttocks myself with tense hands, and went in search of his erect cock. In my haste, I impaled myself with such force that I screamed in pain and slid onto my side, bending my legs. Spellbound by what was happening, Gilles followed my movement passively. I sobbed without tears and he said nothing, didn't move inside me. Then, when the pain stopped, I asked him to move, and he did, gently at first, then more quickly, and it didn't hurt anymore, or only a little, only as much as it had to. I was still lying on my right side when I felt a cramp in my left leg. I asked Gilles to change position. I expected him to come out, but he stayed inside, taking me by the shoulders and tipping me gently onto him. My back was against his chest and belly, my eyes turned to the sky, and his cock stood upright inside me like a pivot. He began to move slowly up and down, thrusting ever so carefully into me, cradling me in his great body, my arms hanging loose, anchored on this rock of flesh. I was drifting ecstatically, drowning, offering up to the sun a spectacle of overwhelming beauty.

There's nothing beautiful about the red-headed man or what he's doing to me. But I like it this way, I like the way his blows accentuate Gilles's gentleness, I like the way his dry, shrill voice makes Gilles's throaty voice ring in my ears, that slightly cracked voice that's the background music to all my emotions, I like the way his brutality deprives me of an orgasm, punishes me where I sin, a depraved little girl whipped for her depravity. That's what I tell myself as he forages inside me and I moan, my head in the pillow, humiliated to the depth of my being—Gilles has my orgasm, Gilles has it all.

The man has stopped. Now he's kissing the back of my neck and my shoulders, with cold, precise little pecks.

Dumbstruck, I wonder what these kisses mean, and the gestures that go with them. He's like a timid adolescent confronted by a girl's naked body, and at the same time, he's manic in his frenzy. This is no lover's frenzy, though.

"You always stay in control, don't you?" I say, hating him.

"Always."

He turns me over with one hand, spreads my legs, and puts his fingers into me. I'm streaming. He laughs.

"You get really wet," he says. "Here, taste."

And he sticks his fingers in my mouth. I don't want to do it. His fingers disgust me, even with the taste of me on them. I hold my breath, and the man notices. Suddenly his teeth start to chatter as if he's cold, his features contort alarmingly, he slaps me hard across the face several times, and his teeth knock together. It's a weird noise, fascinating and terrifying at the same time. There's something wrong with him, I'm sure of that now, he's a madman, the clicking of his teeth indicates the onset of his madness, that and the blows which are getting more and more violent, following one another in a hellish rhythm, sending my head spinning from side to side.

Suddenly, it all stops. The man gives a little groan, goes back to my vulva, puts his fingers inside again, then gives them to me, demanding that I lick them one by one. Holding my breath, I lick, and through my disgust I notice how sharp the taste is, like the sweat of a dying person.

The man has put his head between my legs. He has his tongue in the streaming furrow, drinking the way an exhausted animal drinks, not pausing to take a breath and yet savoring every last drop. Apart from this wet sound, there's a vast silence. The thrusts of his tongue are exact and merciless and unerring. I anticipate them—my cunt has become a mouth, my mucous membranes tastebuds—and my mind, washed free of all fear, walks on the water, my mind is barefoot, a young god newly awakened, and my cunt eats it, then listens to the throbbing of its tiny heartbeat, a fragile little lamp in its red receptacle. My whole existence is there, just as the calm surface of a lake exists only through the sky, the rest of my body has vanished, a neutral landscape, a sterile dune. My body has become empty and inert and useless. Only my cunt is still howling silently, not with that exquisite torture I sometimes feel, which makes me beg for it to be over, but with a peace that eternity itself could not exhaust, like the submissiveness of a kneeling animal, motionless for centuries. When the orgasm arrives—I wasn't expecting it anymore, I was past desire, past hunger—it's nothing like the usual explosion that startles Gilles, when my limbs go stiff and I cry out as if I'm being broken in two. This orgasm is smooth and totally silent, it arches me in a single, slow, unbroken wave, and billions of tiny drops of seawater unite in my veins and on my skin, at the center of my muscles and my nerves. I come like a saint in her ecstasy, radiantly, lips parted in a smile.

"Well, well," the man says. "I thought you were asleep."

I open my eyes. He's lost that twisted look he had, the protruding muscles, the disappearing eyes. His eyes are weary now, and very blue, and his flesh is tender and glistening with sweat. He lies down next to me and relaxes into stillness. His body is like a child's, and his sweat is light as water and has no taste. I drink at the surface of his skin, like a child at its mother's breast.

When we emerge from the red house, the man with the blowtorch looks at us again, and this time I don't lower my eyes. When we emerge from the red house, I'm carrying my orgasm like a pregnant woman her belly, and I want to be shown respect.

3

Sometimes, when Gilles lifts his hand to stroke my face, I quickly shield myself with my arm. The gesture always startles him, as if he's suddenly found himself transported to another planet. We both float for a moment, nauseous, in a state of weightlessness. Then I start to laugh, and the incident is closed.

I have no power over the arm that rises in front of my eyes. Perhaps the simple truth is, I don't want Gilles to touch me anymore. But I can't be sure, about either that or any of the other signs. I eat very little, and only when my body demands it. Sometimes I sleep in the afternoons, curtains drawn against the sun. I get up at night and walk the streets, straight ahead along the canal, until an impulse makes me turn and head back home. Sometimes, when I get back, I find the ginger cat lying on the bed. He looks at me with an air of wild entreaty, as if saying: I love you for the soft bed and the warm room, I love you for the things I've forgotten and the things that are going to happen, I love you for the way your hand touches my fur just like my mother's tongue used to, when I was only a blind, wet ball in a transparent pouch. I chase him away. The following night, he's back. In the end I'll have to keep the window closed.

During the day, I have no desire to move. I stroke Douce and watch the kittens sucking hungrily. Douce is thin, and so am I. I talk to her tenderly. Outside the house, I have no desire to talk. My silence is a tribute to the memory of the blows, a constant longing to be spurned, an obsession with the belly. I can't communicate any of these things, but my silence, my seeming indifference, makes me appear unusually receptive, like an antenna. People have started confiding in me more than they used to. At the agency, the customers take their seats in front of my desk like patients at the doctor's, and the conversations quickly turn confidential. Now I know, as I didn't before, why such and such a person chooses to go to Venice rather than New York. It has nothing to do with the actual cities, or the pictures in the brochures, it has to do with dreams of Venice, dreams of New York, free of all reality. In shops, on the way from the fitting rooms to the cash desk, the assistants tell me their life stories. At the market, a woman told me a recipe for mussels cooked in port, when all I was doing was waiting in line next to her at the fish shop. She was a prodigiously ugly woman, the essence of housewife, with the staleness of daily chores and simmering dishes about her, but those mussels cooked in port gave me a more intimate view of her life than if I had been her best friend, her clairvoyant, or a radio talk-show host she was calling about her personal problems. Maybe I had *become* her for a moment. Not that I found out anything about her personal problems. I was simply present when she showed me the best thing she had to offer, something delicious, a feast for the senses. It was marvelous, like those paper flowers that open when you dip them in water—in a fraction of a second, something closed and stiff reveals itself in all its splendor. I'd like to dip all of humanity in a bath like that, all those stalks of humans who jostle against one another like matches in a closed box.

I've agreed to meet the man a third time, but only because Gilles stood me up. I suspect he did it on purpose, to make me feel nostalgic for what we used to have. Unless it was a misunderstanding, one of those errors of timing that only happen when people are starting to weary of each other. We were supposed to meet outside his sports club. I'd sat down on the stone pillar at the entrance and was swinging my legs, half open, a few centimeters from the ground. I was wearing a short skirt, and above it, a very wide belt that pinched my waist and made my breasts and hips more promi-nent. I think I was almost beautiful.

I waited a long time. People passing ignored me, ex-cept for one old woman who said hello to me. I looked at her. She walked humbly and rather stiffly, the way people do who don't have a succulent fruit between their legs, but a fountain in their heads and fruit in their hearts. I thought of Margot. I returned her greeting, and decided to get up and leave. I'd had enough of waiting for Gilles. My belly felt suddenly empty—the only thing I had left that could help me walk like that woman and greet people with a smile. For a long time, my head and my heart have been pumped dry by my cunt, dissolved by men's hands, my cunt is the one place where my blood still beats, all the rest is dead.

I returned home, wandered around the kitchen for a while, then lay down on my bed with a bottle of beer. I drank the beer straight from the bottle, taking my time, drinking it to the last drop, then lifted my skirt and touched myself for a long time, until I was on the verge of coming. Then I took the empty bottle and thrust it into me, pushing it forward in jerks, as far as I could, but my arm didn't have the strength of Gilles's loins, or the magic, or the madness. I cried out all the same, and arched my body, and when I took the bottle out, the neck was sticky and streaked with white. I licked it. It didn't taste as good as sperm, it was more bitter, slimier, but maybe that was because I was alone and it was my own substance, not the one that Gilles sometimes spurts into my mouth and asks me to keep for a moment before putting it back between his half-open lips, passing it gently from my tongue to his, like a slithery fish.

Gilles never arrived, and the red-headed man phoned. He asked how I was and whether I wanted to see him again. My evasive replies seemed to make him nervous and uncomfortable. His voice grew plaintive as he plied me with questions. Another one, I told myself, who doesn't know the universal law: The more you say, the more you ruin the fantasy.

"I don't suppose," he concluded feverishly, "you want us to meet again?"

I thought about it for a moment or two.

"On one condition. No more blindfolds. I want to see the blows."

"Tomorrow, the one-thirty train," he replied, sounding almost cheerful.

The hotel is a pleasant, middle-class house, the best we've had since the adventure started. The manager looks as sweet and tired as the roses that are shedding their petals on her counter. The buttons you push for the elevator are made of brass, and the sliding door of wood. We go upstairs. The room is huge and clean and overlooks the garden. The eternal drawn curtains bring back childhood memories of English percale. The June sun hammers on the housefront and the windowpanes, making my temples hum. I feel as if I'm going to faint. I sit down in an armchair covered in the same material as the curtains and slowly undress. Once I'm naked, I stand up and, without a word, go to the shower. The towels, hanging on an old-fashioned rail, smell of lavender. I dry myself just a little. The man is waiting for me. I stretch my cool body on the bed, exposing my belly and my chest, my thighs and my face. And I watch.

The eye distances. It captures the promise of pain in the man kneeling beside me, tense, his arm raised, and in the very thin strap of plaited leather which is going to strike, be raised, and fall again, methodically. The eye captures the man's effort, the two horizontal creases on his forehead, the heat that makes him stream with sweat, his growing exhaustion. The quick gestures, the cleanness of the blows, contrast with the infinite wetness of his torso, the blankness of his face. In noting these details, my eyes master the pain, anticipating it, hardening my muscles, so that my flesh, between each sting of the strap, no longer verges on total emptiness, but takes in what comes before and after each blow, all the picturesque details. The man is sweating like a horse being led to the slaughterhouse, and it seems as if his eyes want to say something, there's a mute, desperate message behind those pupils bulging with effort. *I can't help it*, can't help hitting, and you, *you can't help it either*, can't help watching, that's what the man's eyes are saying. By staring at him, I manage not to groan, not to bend my legs, but to leave them extended and slightly open. At each blow, my whole belly vibrates with an invisible contraction. But I remain exposed, seeing each gesture coming, anticipating the distance between the contractions, the decrease in the burning. Giving birth must be like this, the same lucid awareness as you wait for the contraction, the same precise timing that organizes the suffering, breaks it up into almost bearable stages. There are special classes to prepare you for that, lots of big bel-

lies and big chests panting in rhythm, trying hard to re-
duce the future tearing to a matter of cause and effect, to
master its mystery with little narrow controlled breaths,
yes, that's what they teach you, apparently—to control it
all, the anger and the helplessness, the freedom to hit and
bite and cry out like an African woman in labor, to cry
until you find your voice.

I close my eyes now. There's something I still want. It's
the reason I'm here, the reason I'm lying, for the third time,
on a bed in a short-stay hotel. I want to be broken, to be
taken out of the cold once and for all, I want my cry to ring
out, my rage to explode, and my tears to flow. But the man
stops abruptly, and everything stands still. My eyes are still
closed, but I know he's looking at me.

"One of these days," he says, "you're going to dump
me."

I don't reply. I open my eyes. I look in front of me, staring one last time at the darkness of the day. I chew his
wetness as I swallow my saliva. I turn on my side, roll off
the bed, and rush to the shower. I let the ice-cold water
run. My skin crackles as my circulation revives. I am the
most alive thing in the universe, and the coldest. Let the
whole city go up in flames, I don't care. What was the point
in being beaten, showered with insults and sperm, abandoned to a martyr's ecstasy, if not to give me back the very
thing in which I'm at my best, the thing I love and hate—
my cold, chaste body, nourished by an uneventful childhood and the stealthy footsteps of maids?

CAROLINE LAMARCHE

★ ★ ★

By the time we get back on the train, the embankment is already in the shade. The giant hogweed have eaten the sun, cutting the world in two at the level of the buildings, the peeling back walls, the washing lines, the birdcages in the windows. Up above, there is light, while below we ride in darkness.

Tonight I have a crucifix on my belly, purplish and distinct— two lines that have drained off the blood from the blows. I'll have to keep Gilles away. I'll say I have the flu, or my period came early. But the truth is, I haven't heard from him since the day he stood me up. Maybe he's away on a trip. Venice, New York. Far away. Maybe he's gone for good.

It's dark now. I'll sleep through the night, without dreams. But first I'll throw out the ginger cat, if he dares to come into my room again. I'll take him by the spine and shake him, crying: "Get out! Get out! Get out!" three times, like an exorcism. My violence will be painful, like a baby coming out from between my legs. But it will be alive, and it will be hot, so hot that I'll be struck dumb, my face distorted by the cries, disfigured with tears. I'll close the door and the window and cover my head with the sheet, so the animal won't ever come back. I can't feed everybody. I have a boyfriend. Habits. And the sun to worship. That's why I'm sitting at my table tonight, writing to the red-headed

man: "Don't ever come near me again. Ever. Ever. Ever."
I sign it. On the envelope, I put the number of his post office
box. No name. Just the number, the town, and the zip code.
I get up, put on a jacket and sneakers, go to the corner of
the avenue, and throw the letter in the box, just as I would
throw out a stray cat, just as I would bring a new life into
the world—sobbing with pain.

The night will be long and serene.

PASO DOBLE

It's raining.

I'm reminded of my grandfather, who always insisted I go with him on his daily constitutional, even when it rained— not through the woods, as on other days, but around by way of the meadows. When we got to the place where the cows were, he would take my hand and say to them in a polite voice, "Hello! You're so clean today!" To which I would reply, merrily, "That's because of the rain!"

I'm not a little girl anymore. I don't talk on behalf of animals, and nobody holds my hand. I can go out whenever and wherever I like. Today, I've taken a shower, I'm as clean and fresh as a cow in the rain, my lips are moist and my cheeks smooth, I'm wearing a very short skirt under a big black overcoat, and under my panties, there's a moist dew oozing from a very soft patch of hair, that's where I keep my animals now.

I walk quickly, toward the ritzy part of town. When I reach the building, I ring the bell, and without waiting for a reply, I push open the windowed door, cross the small lobby, and climb the stairs two by two to the top floor.

Every time I tell myself: Maybe he's not in, maybe I got the wrong evening, maybe he changed his mind, or he's not alone and won't open the door. But suddenly there he is in front of me, in the doorway of his luxury garret, with the sky eating at the glass roof, the branches of the tree knocking against the panes, and tonight, the rain beating down with rapid little blows.

"You're so solid, so strong, there's such a strength about you," he says.

I hold him tight against me, and think about her, the woman with slender wrists and ankles. Her wrists, her ankles, her very long neck, her hips—you can see through the dress how narrow they are—are all on the photo stuck to the refrigerator door in the kitchen. And there's another photo on the table in the living room. *Paso doble!* he says, drawing me in.

There's always music at his place. As soon as I've entered, I'm free to sway, to go with the rhythm. He moves in step, he's a good mover, and I follow, trying my best to be sexy, that's what I always have to be, sexy, to please him, otherwise I'd be straight back out in the cold and the rain with no one to hold my hand.

"Let yourself go," he says, "we're in Spain, the Gypsy girls dance like goddesses, they have big breasts and they arch their backs so you can see their pubes, and when they fuck, it's seven orgasms an hour, one explosion after another, like a witch's cauldron. *Paso doble*, dance!"

He clings to me though I'm no dancer, and the living room is transformed into a Spanish bar where beautiful

Gypsy girls watch me and laugh. He goes off with three of them, and I stay there in the rain, the rain of a season that will pass like every other season.

Later, in the kitchen, I watch him eating by himself. "Don't worry about me," I told him, "I'm not hungry." That's what I always say, and he obeys me, never makes me anything to eat. I sit opposite him and drink a glass of wine. He's wearing one of the twenty-five beautiful shirts the woman with the slender wrists and ankles has bought him. He has broad shoulders, a neat waist, and long legs that clasp mine. I tell myself that we're married, even if it isn't true. Because I watch him eat, because his legs hold mine like a padlock, I'm his wife, forever. We'll have children together and lead them through the meadows to see the cows in the rain.

He's just finishing his meal when the telephone rings. It doesn't always rain, the wind doesn't always push the branches of the tree up against the windowpane, but the phone always rings. I'm allowed to stay where I am, I'm not in the way. I leave the table, take a book from the library, and go and lie down on the carpet. I peer over the top of the book and see his feet pacing the carpet, his shoes, well polished as always, his English socks—he doesn't buy them himself, the woman owns a men's clothing store. I imagine him sitting in a closed cubicle, barefoot, and her on her knees, with her skirt lifted as far as her navel and her transparent groin exposed, slipping an English sock on his foot, a sock as soft as a vagina.

He's talking to her on the phone. I can't hear what he's saying because of the storm inside my head, I can only see his lips moving, imploring, and his eyes searching for me. "Stay with us," his eyes say when they meet mine. "Stay, you're so strong."

Afterwards, he hangs up the receiver and lies down next to me.

"Did you hear how I comforted her, how I told her to be brave?"

He snuggles up in my arms. He's like a child with a fever, unable to keep still.

"Is she going to leave her husband soon?" I ask him gently. "Will she be able to live here with you?"

"I don't know," he says. "It's so hard, it's been such a long time, we're so alone, she and I, alone against the whole world."

He begins to cry, desperately.

I stroke his face, and in the same insistent rhythm as the rain, I say these few words:

"I'm with the two of you, against the whole world."

★ ★ ★

The tree rubs against the window, the rain lubricates the glass.

He has stretched me on the bed. He takes off my shoes, then strokes my hair, pulling it back.

"Your forehead is like a little girl's."

His fingers brush against my wrist and loosen my watch. It slides off and falls to the floor.

There's a lamp beside the bed. And under the lamp, always something of *hers*.

The first time, a letter, written in a fine hand, that began "*My love* . . ."

I didn't read the rest.

The second time, a tuft of very black pubic hair on a sheet of white paper. It had been cut with scissors.

Sometimes it's a wristwatch. Left by accident.

And today?

Today, there's nothing under the lamp.

But when I'm lying down and he's taking off my skirt, skinning me like a freshly killed rabbit, I notice a diagonal shadow on the ceiling, shaped almost like a snout.

I sit up. There's a pair of women's panties on the lampshade.

I say nothing. I lie down again and wait.

He bends over me.

"Take that away!" I shout.

He raises himself on his elbows, reaches out his arm, and grabs the panties. They're white with little garnet flowers and a little flat garnet knot at the front. He places the panties over his face and shakes his head slowly, so as not to drop them.

He laughs. "I haven't washed them."

I change my mind. "Leave them," I say, at my most charming, "it doesn't matter." Then, imploring: "Promise me there'll always be something of hers when I come here."

"I promise," he says, placing the trophy under the lamp. "You see, I forgot all about it today. It's lucky you reminded me."

He lies down on top of me. His voice is soft now, as soft as his skin. "I know you by heart, you're as tense as a little girl, you don't move, you don't cry out, you never will. She cries out, if you only knew how she cries out!"

He sits up and looks at me, then changes my position. My left arm extended, my right arm over my eyes, my legs separated but bent, my feet placed flat on the carpet. He has plenty of room. He sits down cross-legged, naked now, a yogi meditating. He takes a deep breath, like a diver getting ready.

He takes the plunge. His fingers are inside me. Without looking at me, he concentrates on his hand as it opens me and searches around and is swallowed, with a squelchy octopus sound, and then comes out again, shining and wet like my grandfather's hand when he stroked the muzzle of his favorite cow. The other cows would breathe loudly, then move away with worried looks in their eyes, but that one would let herself be approached without flinching and put out a humid tongue and swallow his fingers thoughtfully.

"She . . ." he says, stretching me beneath him.

He rolls his beautiful shirt under me, one of the twenty-five.

"You."

His voice has changed, it's like a knife cutting into a piece of meat, cutting quickly before the meat gets cold and loses all its blood.

"You," he says, "you."

He talks like that sometimes, strongly, urgently, like a hungry ogre, a surgeon preventing a hemorrhage, a vampire who has to be finished before sunrise.

He enters me, fucks me hard and deep. My head bangs against the wall.

"She," he says, slowly withdrawing.

"And you," he says, thrusting in again so violently I feel as if I'm going to die.

He is silent now, plowing his way in like a stranger, his despair focused on them, him and her, two people united— thanks to me—against the whole world.

"Don't cry out!" his voice commands.

I lock up my cry, I kill it, in homage to the woman with the slender wrists and ankles, who dances better and fucks better than me.

Then, all at once, because I've been silent so long, a great passive silent body letting itself be moved, I come at last into a boundless light, and my limbs catch fire and fly off with a great beating of wings while he cries out and falls.

★ ★ ★

He drifts off to sleep, a heavy sleep like a child's, with my leg trapped beneath his. When it hurts too much, I move a little, but he feels it, and half awake, he presses harder until I'm still again. I turn to look at the window. It's pouring down, rivulets are forming, all the waters are joining together, the branches rub against the panes, cows are looking at us and mooing dully. How clean they are today, Grandpa.

That's because of the rain.

THE ISLAND

They have been walking around downtown for quite a while. Elsa has bought two pairs of shorts, a blue one for the older girl, a pink one for the younger, and a book for each. She has pointed out the old guitarist, the one who stands in the arcade and is given coins of twenty or fifty, and even bills of one hundred, by people passing by, their hearts swelling with gratitude for so many cheerful tunes. Now she has taken them to a McDonald's, and they've chosen to go upstairs, sitting down with their burgers and Cokes next to a stained-glass window. The view is partly obscured by a flag with the McDonald's sign, but whenever the flag moves aside in the breeze, they can see a swarthy little boy sitting barefoot on the sidewalk, with a tin can in front of him, and on his knees a piece of cardboard with something written on it. From this angle, they can't read what it says. The boy is so dirty they can see brown streaks on his face. Elsa remembers the poster she glanced at this morning at the baker's, advertising a lecture called "Your skin, a major asset" and a free demonstration of cosmetic products. She explains to her daughters that a blackened face is one of the major assets of a street kid—it's what you show people when you can't sing or play an instrument to attract the public. She thinks it's a good thing to open the eyes of her well-to-do girls to such realities. A walk downtown can be very instructive when you live in a residential suburb that looks like a very clean stretch of countryside, with well-kept roads. Besides, Elsa tells herself as she watches her daughters eating their burgers, compassion comes easy to them. So she places two coins next to their glasses, one for each. "Don't forget to give it to the little boy on the way out!"

Two tables away from them, a fat young man with bulging eyes is sitting. He's eating without looking at anyone. Elsa wonders what kind of thoughts can possibly be buried beneath that pile of fat. She supposes that from where he's sitting—facing the second window—he can also see the little beggar boy and the flag flapping like an unfurled sail. But all he's looking at is his burger. Even then he's looking at it without seeing it, totally absorbed in the act of eating, with what seems a kind of morose contempt, a despair at not seeing, not feeling, not tasting anything through the prison of fat—at least, that's how Elsa interprets it, and she knows what she's talking about, she thinks, because as a teenager she, too, went though a phase when she was bulimic and had a kind of gray hatred of the world. But right now, she has no memory of it, or rather her memory isn't an obstacle anymore, and it seems curious to her that, even though you know perfectly well what you were, you can be affected by a kind of amnesia of the senses, so that you can't relive what you felt in the past, and you're reduced to imagining despair, the way someone imagined one day that it might be a good idea to put chopped meat into soft rolls or to fit stained glass in a McDonald's window. She is overwhelmed with contentment at the thought that the past can disappear as quickly as the mouthfuls of a meal you scarf down without thinking. She realizes now why she burned the poet's letters. Everything vanished so quickly, a little bundle of ashes that immediately grew cold. She thinks now it was the right thing to do—there's no point in thinking about him anymore. A day will come, in fact, when the only thing she'll have left will be to *imagine* everything that happened, as if that man with his fiery eyes, who looked like a retired government employee in his worn suit, had never spoken to her in the tearoom where she was taking a rest from her shopping, as if he had not sat down next to her without hesitating and begun reading her one of his own poems, as if she had not succumbed to the charm of his words, had not agreed to see him again and let him write to her without her husband knowing but on a purely platonic basis. The letters were innocent enough—he talked about the taste of the air and the sound of the rain, about Verlaine and Lorca— and there were more poems, too, poems in praise of Woman, Her role as muse, as inspiration, as glorious oracle.

It was all a dream, she thinks now, just one more dream among other dreams—most are still to come, they can rise up at any moment, anything can set them off, a child's gaze, a glass of Coke, a piece of stained glass. Yes, Elsa tells herself with intense excitement, I'm a factory of dreams . . . and right now she is transported in her imagination into a fault in the stained glass, a bubble of air inadvertently trapped in the pane. She stares at it unblinking for a while, until her eyes smart. Then she looks away, and the whole room seems red. The girls have bloodshot eyes, as if they are on a photo taken with a flash, and the food is red, and the napkins and the plastic knives and forks. For a moment Elsa is enchanted. Then sadness comes over her like a wave. The poet wrote to her in red ink. Obviously it's not enough for her to transport herself into a bubble of air and dream to her heart's content, she can't forget so easily all about that handwriting the color of fresh blood—or about the red dress she was wearing the day she was raped.

It happened when their correspondence was at its height. One day, Elsa was walking along a path in an almost deserted part of the park, waiting for her daughters to come out of school, when a stranger with a hood over his face emerged from the bushes, clutching a knife. "Don't move, don't scream!" The man placed the point of the knife in the hollow of Elsa's neck, against the jugular, and dragged her clumsily to a damp hollow, where he ordered her to undress. Her legs quaking, she took off her red dress and lay down, still under the threat of the knife. Her mind bolted like a frightened horse, and she began to moan crazily, shaking her head from side to side, her mouth filling with dead leaves. "Drop the knife . . . drop the knife . . ." she begged endlessly, the words gushing from her lips and throat and belly, all the time, all the time that he . . .

Forget. Leave the stained-glass window, transport yourself into the street, keep your eyes on the crowd, let yourself be divided by the crowd, into little fragments of faces and hair and hands and knees. There's a store down there with clothes hanging on a rail near the entrance and women fingering them, taking them down. So reassuring, so banal. Buying something to attract glances—she used to dream of that. Not now. Now all she wants is to pass unnoticed, she doesn't care if men never look at her again. Let her daughters attract all the attention, her beautiful daughters with their swollen lips and hair as smooth as silk. The poet was in his sixties, but his desire for women was as strong as ever. For her, all that is over. She looks through the window without emotion, at this town like so many others, neither more nor less busy, with its beggars lying in the same positions as everywhere else. And yet this street is not just any street. She often walked along it with the poet. It was all quite innocent—she might have been with her own father. He never touched her. Just a peck on the cheek, like a friend or a well-behaved child. But he liked the red dress.

"Mummy, what's the little beggar boy doing?"

"Nothing—just waiting."

"You're watching him, aren't you?"

"You can see she's watching him," the older girl says to the younger, who is drawing on the table with a finger dipped in ketchup.

Elsa's gaze returns to the window. She looks down. All she wants is to vanish utterly into the mobile heart of the crowd and scatter happily with them in all directions, the past flowing away beneath everyone's feet like an underground stream, she wants this particular street to be like any other street in any other town, so that it could lead even to the sea like a river turned toward the setting sun, while the hamburgers and the flag and the glasses and the plastic forks and even the pieces of stained glass have long since drowned along with the housefronts and the paving stones, the people in the restaurant and the people on the street . . . Her forehead against the windowpane, Elsa breathes methodically, to the rhythm of an imaginary march. She is heading for the open sea, for the sun of oblivion.

At this exact moment, the sun goes down. Just like a picture postcard. A card showing the mouth of the river, the waves and the setting sun—a piece of card curling at the edges, like the rest, in the auto-da-fé she lit to exorcise the past. There are words written on the back, in red ink: "The river joins the sea. The wind pants and flees, guilty of the disorder on the beach . . ." Elsa holds her breath, staring stupidly at the lead frames of the stained-glass window. No image, no daydream escapes the poet. His power did not vanish when his letters dissolved in ashes. Even today Elsa drowns in that scarlet ink, her lungs are full of it, even the air she breathes. There's no escape. There isn't a single crack in the sidewalk, a single centimeter of skin, a single fold in a garment, a single fiber of her memory that does not contain red, that does not recall the rape and the poet.

Back to the street, look again at humanity in motion, humanity pounding on the sidewalk like rain. The stream, denser now with people coming out of offices, moves quickly, a uniform mass, except for one white spot, pitching like a skiff tossed by the waves—a woman in a veil, a